Old Mother Goose,
    When she wanted to wander,
Would ride through the air
    On a very fine gander.

Rain, rain, go away,
Come again another day,
Little Johnny wants to play.

It's raining, it's pouring,
The old man's snoring;
He got into bed
And bumped his head
And couldn't get up in the morning.

Knock on the door,
Peek in.
Lift up the latch,
And walk in.

Tickly, tickly, on your knee,
If you laugh you don't love me.

Baa, baa, black sheep,
Have you any wool?
Yes, sir, yes, sir,
Three bags full;
One for the master,
And one for the dame,
And one for the little boy
Who lives down the lane.

Humpty Dumpty sat on a wall,
Humpty Dumpty had a great fall;
All the king's horses and all the King's men
Couldn't put Humpty together again.

Pat-a-cake, pat-a-cake, baker's man,
Bake me a cake as fast as you can;
Pat it and prick it, and mark it with T,
Put it in the oven for Tommy and me.

Great A, little a,
Bouncing B,
The cat's in the cupboard
And can't see me.

Dickery, dickery, dare,
The pig flew up in the air;
The man in brown
Soon brought him down,
Dickery, dickery, dare.

Little Boy Blue,
Come blow your horn,
The sheep's in the meadow,
The cow's in the corn.
Where is the boy
Who looks after the sheep?
He's under a haystack,
Fast asleep.

1, 2,
Buckle my shoe;

3, 4,
Knock at the door;

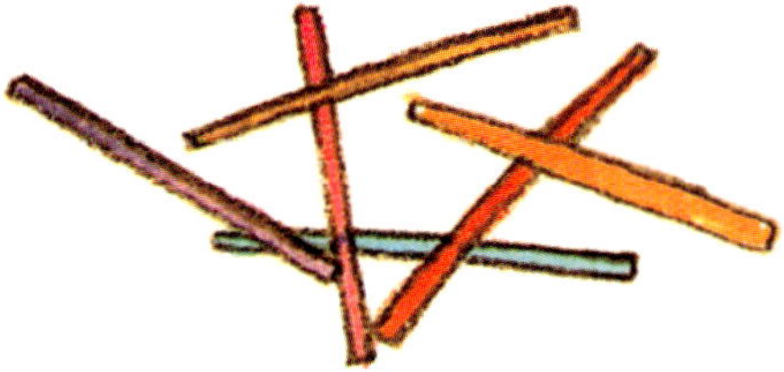

5, 6
Pick up sticks;

7,8
Lay them straight;

9, 10,
A big fat hen.

Ring-a-ring o'roses,
A pocket full of posies,
A-tishoo! A-tishoo!
We all fall down.

The cows are in the meadow
Lying fast asleep,
A-tishoo! A-tishoo!
We all get up again.

Rub-a-dub-dub,
Three men in a tub,
The butcher, the baker,
The candlestick-maker.

Little Miss Muffet
Sat on a tuffet,
Eating her curds and whey;
There came a big spider,
Who sat down beside her
And frightened Miss Muffet away.

Here am I,
Little Jumping Joan;
When nobody's with me,
I'm all alone.

Jack be nimble,
Jack be quick,
Jack jump over
The candlestick.

Mary, Mary, quite contrary,
How does your garden grow?
With silver bells and cockle shells,
And pretty maids all in a row.

Diddle, diddle, dumpling, my son John,
Went to bed with his trousers on;
One shoe off, and one shoe on,
Diddle, diddle, dumpling, my son John.

This little pig went to market,
This little pig stayed home,
This little pig had roast beef,
This little pig had none,
And this little pig cried, Wee-wee-
    wee-wee-wee,
I can't find my way home.

See-saw, Margery Daw,
Jacky shall have a new master;
Jacky shall have but a penny a day,
Because he can't work any faster.

Roses are red,
Violets are blue,
Sugar is sweet
And so are you.

As Tommy Snooks and Bessy Brooks
Were walking out one Sunday,
Says Tommy Snooks to Bessy Brooks,
Tomorrow will be Monday.

Three little kittens
They lost their mittens,
And they began to cry,
Oh, Mother dear,
We sadly fear
Our mittens we have lost.
What!  lost your mittens,
You naughty kittens!
Then you shall have no pie.
Mee-ow, mee-ow, mee-ow.
No, you shall have no pie.

The three little kittens
They found their mittens,
And they began to cry,
Oh, Mother dear,
See here, see here,
Our mittens we have found.
Put on your mittens,
You silly kittens,
And you shall have some pie.
Purr-r, purr-r, purr-r,
Oh, let us have some pie.

Yanke Doodle came to town,
Riding on a pony;
He stuck a feather in his cap
And called it macaroni.

Pussy cat, pussy cat,
Where have you been?
I've been to London
To look at the Queen.
Pussy cat, pussy cat,
What did you there?
I frightened a little mouse
Under her chair.

Hot cross buns, hot cross buns;
One a penny poker,
Two a penny tongs,
Three a penny fire shovel,
Hot cross buns.

There was an old woman
who lived in a shoe,
She had so many children,
she didn't know what to do.

Chook, chook, chook, chook, chook,
Good morning, Mrs. Hen.
How many chickens have you got?
Madam, I've got ten.
Four of them are yellow,
And four of them are brown,
And two of them are speckled red,
The nicest in the town.

Hush-a-bye, baby, on the tree top,
When the wind blows the cradle will rock;
When the bough breaks the cradle will fall,
Down will come baby, cradle, and all.

Wee Willie Winkie runs through the town,
Upstairs and downstairs in his night-gown,
Rapping at the window, crying through the lock,
Are the children all in bed, for now it's eight o'clock?

I see the moon,
And the moon sees me;
God bless the moon,
And God bless me.